Walt Disney

Lady and the Tramp

A WALT DISNEY CLASSIC

PURNELL
London, W. 1

IT was on Christmas Eve that Lady came to live with her People, Jim Dear and Darling. They loved her at once, but as often happens they needed some training from her.

For example, they thought she would like a little bed and blankets of her own. It took some howls and whines from Lady to show them their mistake. But it was not long before they understood that her place was at the feet of either Jim Dear or Darling. People are really quite intelligent, as every dog knows. It just takes a little patience to make them understand.

By the time spring arrived, Lady had everything under control. Every morning she wakened Jim Dear with a bark and a lick at his hand, brought his slippers and waited till he got up.

Then out she raced, through her own small swinging door, to meet the postman at the gate. After the postman came the paper-boy, and then it was time for breakfast.

After making certain that Darling did not need her help with the housework, Lady went out. She had two close friends of her own, who

lived in the houses on either side of hers. One was an old Scotsman, known to his friends as Jock. The other was a fine, dignified old bloodhound, Trusty by name. Lady, Jock and Trusty spent many happy days playing together.

Perhaps the very nicest part of Lady's day came towards the evening, when Jim Dear came home from work. Lady would fly to meet him at

his whistle, and scamper home at his side. Then the family of three was together again—Jim Dear, Darling and Lady. At this moment of the day Lady felt the happiest dog in the world.

It was autumn that year when a stranger came to the district where Lady lived. He was a cheeky young mongrel known simply as the Tramp. This day he was two jumps ahead of the dog catcher's net, as he

rounded the corner near Lady's house. Just then along the street came a stately open carriage, followed by two proud carriage hounds. The Tramp fell into step with the two proud hounds until he saw the dog catcher give up the chase in disgust. Then he left the procession.

"Well," he thought, "I may as well have a look around the district as long as I'm here."

And his feet led him down the shady street to the house where Lady lived with her People.

At that very minute, Lady was telling a very important piece of news to Trusty and Jock—Darling was going to have a baby!

"A baby!" barked Jock. "A baby means a . . ."

". . . Lot of trouble," a new voice broke in. It was the Tramp, who now swaggered up to join the group. "Babies scratch, pinch and pull ears," he went on to say, "but any dog can take that. It's what they do to your happy home! Just you wait, Miss. You'll see what happens when that baby gets here. A human heart has only so much room for love and affection, and when a baby moves in—the dog moves out!"

Poor Lady! She had a long time to worry—all through the long dreary winter months. At last, on a night of wind and rain, in a most confusing flurry, the baby came.

Now there was a stranger in Lady's old room. Lady was scarcely allowed inside the door. And when she did follow Darling in, all she could see was a small, high bed and a strange, wrapped-up shape in Darling's arms. But there was a smile on Jim Dear's lips and a new softness in Darling's eyes, so Lady began to think there must be something nice about the baby after all. If only they could be friends and play! Perhaps it might have worked out that way soon if only Jim Dear had not been called away.

"I'll only be gone a few days," Jim Dear explained to Lady. Aunt Sarah will be here to help you, and I'm counting on you to . . ."

Knock! Knock!

The door shook under a torrent of bangs. It was Aunt Sarah. Lady watched from between Jim Dear's legs as a stern-faced lady marched in, leaving a stack of luggage on the doorstep for Jim Dear to bring in.

"I'll put your bags away for you, Aunt Sarah," Jim offered.

"No need for that.

You just hurry up, James, or you'll miss your train," ordered Aunt Sarah in a bossy voice.

"Oh—er, all right, Aunt Sarah," Jim Dear said. As he rushed out of the door he managed a last pat for Lady. "It's going to be a little rough for a while," it meant, "but I'm counting on you to watch over things for me."

Lady knew her job. She raced upstairs to the bed where Darling was having a rest and snuggled down on the coverlet beside her.

Not for long, though.

"What is that animal doing here?" Aunt

Sarah's voice demanded loudly as she appeared in the doorway.

"Oh, it's just Lady," Darling smiled.

"Get off that bed," snapped Aunt Sarah—and she pushed Lady. "You'll get fleas on the baby! Shoo! Shoo!"

Poor Lady! She was hustled straight out of the room, back down the stairs to the front hall. There, still waiting on the doorstep, stood all Aunt Sarah's bags. Lady gave them an experimental sniff.

There was something very peculiar about one basket—a smell unfamiliar to Lady, and one she did not understand. She sniffed again, and circled the basket.

Zip! Out shot a silken paw and clawed her from behind.

Lady pounced on the basket. Suddenly, out sprang two large forms! Cats—two Siamese cats! That really was the end of Lady's peaceful, happy life.

The cats were sly, they were sleek, they were tricky as could be. They walked across the mantelpiece, scratched the best table legs and bounced on the cushions Lady never touched—but whenever Aunt Sarah came into the room, they made it seem that Lady had done everything bad while they had behaved like twin angels!

"Get away, little beast!" Aunt Sarah would say, kicking at Lady with a toe. "Poor darlings," she would coo then, scooping up the Siamese

cats in her arms. "Dogs don't belong in the house with you!"

Poor Lady! She was blamed for trying to catch the goldfish, when in fact she was just protecting them from the cats. And when the cats opened the canary cage and were chasing the poor frightened little bird—guess who got the blame from Aunt Sarah? Yes, poor Lady again, of course!

Aunt Sarah even put her out at night, in the rain. Everything was just as bad as the Tramp had said it would be—if not worse! Oh, what a sad, sad life!

Little though Lady knew it, an even more dreadful thing was still to happen. One day, Aunt Sarah took Lady into the city to the pet shop and bought her a muzzle.

"It isn't safe to have this beast around unmuzzled, with a baby in the house,"

she said. Tears filled poor Lady's eyes. Then Aunt Sarah snapped the muzzle on to her.

"There now, you little brute!" said Aunt Sarah.

Lady could stand no more. She had put up with the sly tricks of the cats, the scoldings from Aunt Sarah—she had even suffered being put out in the cold and the dark and the rain without so much as a whine of protest. But a muzzle was the last straw! Even for a gentle, good-natured little dog like Lady, there was a time to rebel.

So Lady hurled herself forward, wrenching as hard as she could at her lead. It was no use. Aunt Sarah's grip was too firm.

"Stop that pulling, you horrid little dog!" she snapped.

Lady whirled round then, grabbing the lead in her mouth. She reared back on her strong little legs and with one mighty tug freed herself from Aunt Sarah. Then away she ran, as fast as she could go.

"Lady! Lady! Come back here at once!" shrieked Aunt Sarah. Lady was sure she was pursuing her, and ran all the faster.

Luckily, the pavements were crowded with people, so there were lots of legs for Lady to dodge in between as she ran. It made it very difficult for Aunt Sarah to catch her. In fact, she gave up almost at once but Lady did not know that. She kept on running and running.

At last she had to pause and pant for breath. Only then did she realize what she had done. Here she was, lost in the middle of the city and without the faintest idea of how to get home! She sat down miserably on the pavement and looked around for a familiar tree, or gate or lamp-post. She saw nothing at all she recognized. What was more, she was being kicked and trodden on by all the hurrying, scurrying careless feet.

So Lady got up again and walked on. She thought that if she just kept on walking for long enough she might even arrive at the road where she lived.

After she had been walking for some time, Lady found that the streets were getting smaller and quieter. Less feet jostled her, and less wheels clattered noisily past. At any other time she would have been interested in all the fresh smells and sights and sounds around her, but just then she was too unhappy to care. And too weary. Lady's legs were

strong but they were short, and she had come a long way from home.

How she longed to be back in her own yard, with her two dear friends Trusty and Jock!

At last, tired out and frightened, Lady trotted down a dim, quiet alleyway and found a place to rest and hide behind a big barrel. There

she lay and shook with fear and exhaustion.

"Well, pigeon, what are you doing here?" she heard a brisk voice say.

It was the Tramp, and how handsome he looked to Lady, how big and strong! Trustingly she told him the whole sad story, ending with a sob, "And now I don't know what to do next."

"First of all we've got to get rid of that contraption," said the Tramp, with a nod at her muzzle. "Let's see—a knife? No, that's for humans. Scissors? Saw? Teeth? That's what we need, teeth! Come on, we'll visit the zoo."

Lady had never heard of a zoo, but she obediently followed the Tramp along. And she did just as the Tramp told her to, until they were safely

past the NO DOGS sign, strolling down the sunny paths.
Never in her wildest dreams had Lady imagined that animals
came in such a variety of shapes, sizes and colours. But though
all of them were nice about it, there did not seem to be one

animal who could help—until they came to the Beaver house.

"That's a pretty harness," Beaver said, pointing to Lady's muzzle.

"We were hoping you could help us get it off," the Tramp explained.

"Well, the only way I can do that is by chewing through it, and that seems a shame . . ."

"That's exactly what we had in mind," grinned the Tramp.

"It is?" The Beaver was surprised. "Well, it's your thingummyjig. Hold still now. This may hurt a bit."

Lady kept as still as she could, and in a few moments she was free.

"It's off! It's off!" cried Lady. "Oh, thank you, thank you," she stopped to say, as the Tramp prepared to lead her away.

As they looked back, the Beaver was trying on the muzzle with a happy smile on his face.

"What do you want to do now, pigeon?" the Tramp asked.

"Oh, I'll have to go home now," Lady said.

"Home?" said the Tramp. "You'll just find yourself in another muzzle. Have dinner with me in a little place I know, then I'll show you the town."

Lady found herself following along, and she had to admit that dinner on the back step of a little restaurant was the best meal she'd had for weeks. Afterwards they went to the circus—Lady's first— where they had wonderful seats under the front row.

Then came a stroll in the park, and since it was spring, the night was warm and they were young, time passed all too quickly. The first rays of morning took Lady by surprise.

"Oh, dear!" she exclaimed. "The baby . . . I must go home."

The Tramp argued, but Lady insisted and so they set off. But on the way they passed a chicken yard. The Tramp could not resist.

"Ever chased chickens?" he asked. "No? You've never lived." In a flash, he was scraping a hole under the fence. When Lady said they shouldn't do it, the Tramp replied, "That's why it's fun!"

So she followed him in; but when the chickens squawked and the farmer came running, it was Lady who was caught. The next thing she knew, she was in the Dog Pound—and among very strange companions. At first they frightened her, but soon she learned they had hearts of gold. And they all knew the Tramp.

"Now there's a bloke what never gets caught," said one admiringly. Another agreed with him.

"His only weakness is the ladies," he said. "Got a new one every week."

Lady felt very sad then. She was sure the Tramp had let her be caught so he could take up with another girl.

When she arrived home, she did not feel any better. She was put out in the dog house, on a stout chain.

When the Tramp came to call next, Lady could not even speak to him. That pleased one grey figure lurking in the woodpile. The grey figure was that arch-enemy of all society—the Rat.

For years the Rat had poked around the yard, trying to find a way into the house. But always he had been frightened off by the thought of a dog on guard. Now, seeing Lady safely chained up and having watched her send the Tramp away, the Rat thought his big chance had come

at last! In the dim light of dusk, he left his hiding-place and scurried towards the back door.

Lady saw the sly figure, and instinct told her this creature was evil. She barked wildly, and far down the street the Tramp heard. Upstairs, Aunt Sarah heard too.

"Stop that racket!" she shouted.

Meanwhile the evil Rat was slinking

quietly up the stairs. But at that moment, too, the Tramp came back.

"A horrible creature . . . in the house," Lady panted. "The baby . . .!"

With a desperate lunge she broke the chain and raced fearlessly for the back door. Through the kitchen the Tramp and Lady raced, side by side in the darkness; then into the hall and up the stairs. Lady led the way into the baby's room then both stopped short; there, sure enough, was the Rat!

The Tramp knew exactly what to do. He disposed of the Rat and was returning, still panting from his battle, when Aunt Sarah appeared.

"Take that, you mangy cur!" she cried,

lashing out with her broom. The Tramp winced and ran—and a moment later found himself locked in a very dark cupboard!

Now Darling was in the baby's room, cuddling the baby. "Lady," she said in surprise, "whatever got into you?"

"It's plain enough!" said Aunt Sarah. "She brought one of her vicious friends in to attack the baby."

"Oh, I'm sure she wouldn't!" cried Darling.

"Rubbish!" said Aunt Sarah. "Tomorrow I'll get rid of that other brute for good. And as for you . . ." She picked Lady up by the scruff of her neck and threw her out.

Bad news travels fast, and by morning Jock and Trusty

knew what the Tramp's fate was to be. They watched as the dog catcher came to take him to his doom.

"If only we could think of some way to help!" said Jock.

Then a wonderful thing happened. A taxi stopped at the door, and Jim

Dear climbed out. He was home at last! Darling greeted him with the story of their terrible night, and he was puzzled.

"Why should Lady . . ." he began, when Lady jumped past him and raced upstairs. She showed him what lay behind a chair in the baby's room.

"Darling!" cried Jim. "That strange dog wasn't attacking the baby! He was helping Lady to protect it!"

"Oh, Jim Dear, and we've sent him to be . . ." Darling wailed.

"I don't see the reason for this fuss," Aunt Sarah said sternly.

"Aunt Sarah, I'm going to save that dog," said Jim. "And when I come home, I trust you will be ready to leave!"

Jim Dear was as good as his word. He brought the Tramp home in a taxicab, and by that time Aunt Sarah had her bags packed—cats and all! She left the house with her head in the air, and none of them ever saw her again.

So the happy little family was re-united, but with one addition to their number—the Tramp! And, in fact, that family grew and grew. By the time the baby was crawling around the floor, there were five cuddly little puppies for it to play with. Four proud parents were there, looking on in delight; Jim Dear and Darling—and, of course, Lady and the Tramp.